PEANUTS®
Holiday Treasury

LITTLE SIMON
New York   London   Toronto   Sydney

TABLE OF CONTENTS

It's the Great Pumpkin, Charlie Brown

By Charles M. Schulz
Adapted by Justine and Ron Fontes
Art adapted by Paige Braddock
Based on the television special produced by Lee Mendelson and Bill Melendez

Dear Great Pumpkin,
I'm looking forward to seeing you on Halloween night. I hope you will bring me lots of presents....

Every year Linus writes to the Great Pumpkin. And every year he waits in the most sincere pumpkin patch he can find, hoping to see his mysterious hero.

"On Halloween night the Great Pumpkin rises out of his pumpkin patch and flies through the air with his bag of toys for all the children," Linus explained to Charlie Brown.

"You must be crazy," Charlie Brown said.

Linus's sister, Lucy, cried, "Writing to the Great Pumpkin again? You'll make me the laughing stock of the neighborhood!"

Linus sighed. "There are three things I've learned never to discuss with people: religion, politics, and the Great Pumpkin."

11

Sally was the only one who didn't laugh at Linus. "You say the cutest things," she said.

"Would you like to join me in the pumpkin patch this year?" Linus asked.

Sally smiled. "Oh, I'd love to."

Linus was excited! This Halloween he would have company in the pumpkin patch. And surely this time the Great Pumpkin would appear! But first Linus had to mail his letter.

Nearby, Charlie Brown opened his own mailbox. For once, it wasn't empty.

"I got an invitation to a Halloween party!" Charlie Brown danced with joy. "I've never gotten a party invitation before."

"Is it Violet's party?" Lucy asked. "Your name must have wound up on the wrong list. You were on the *don't invite* list."

When Sally heard about the party she asked, "Is Linus taking me?" She wanted to go to the party, but she wanted to be with her "sweet baboo" even more.

"My blockhead brother is out in the pumpkin patch making his yearly fool of himself," Lucy grumbled.

"Boy, is he strange," Violet agreed. "Missing all the fun."

"Maybe there is a Great Pumpkin," Sally said, defending her sweetheart.

But Sally soon forgot about the Great Pumpkin. Everybody was getting ready for Halloween. All the kids were making ghost costumes, except Lucy.

"Where's Charlie Brown?" Schroeder wondered aloud.

"Here I am," Charlie Brown said from under a sheet full of holes. "I had a little trouble with the scissors."

Everyone recognized Pigpen by his cloud of dust. But there was one strange figure in the crowd.

"Who in the world is that?" Lucy asked when she saw Snoopy's costume.

"He's a World War I Flying Ace," Charlie Brown explained.

Flying Ace or no Flying Ace, Lucy decided to take charge. "All right. First we'll go trick-or-treating. Then we'll go to Violet's party," she declared as the World War I Ace slipped off into the night.

17

Linus was waiting at the pumpkin patch when the rest of the gang walked by.
"Have you come to sing pumpkin carols?" he asked.
"Blockhead! You're going to miss the fun again," Lucy said.
"Don't talk like that!" Linus exclaimed. "The Great Pumpkin will come because I am in the most sincere pumpkin patch."

"Oh, good grief!" Lucy marched off with the ghosts.
Sally went along. But at the last minute, she ran back.

Linus grinned. "You'll see the Great Pumpkin with your own eyes! The Great Pumpkin has to pick this patch. I don't see how a pumpkin patch could be more sincere than this."

Linus wasn't trick-or-treating, but he wasn't forgotten. "Can I have extra candy for my stupid brother?" Lucy demanded at each house. "He couldn't come with us because he's waiting for the Great Pumpkin."

"It's so embarrassing," Lucy sighed.

"I got a chocolate bar," Pigpen reported.

"I got a quarter!" Schroeder added.

"I got a rock," Charlie Brown said.

No one noticed that Snoopy was missing.

Snoopy had gone off by himself and climbed on top of his doghouse. He pretended it was a World War I airplane.

Ra-ta-ta-ta-ta-ta-tat!
The World War I Flying Ace fired his machine guns.
Ra-ta-ta-ta-ta-ta-tat!
The Red Baron fired back!
Curse you Red Baron!
The brave pilot went down with his plane.

22

The World War I Flying
Ace sneaked off into the
night behind enemy lines.
He took shelter where he
could, but always pressed
on toward his goal.

On their way to Violet's house the gang stopped at the pumpkin patch. They couldn't believe Sally was going to miss the party.

"Just wait until the Great Pumpkin comes," Sally shouted. "Linus knows what he's doing. The Great Pumpkin will be here!"

But Sally was beginning to have her doubts. As soon as the other kids left, Sally turned to Linus and shouted, "All right, where is this Great Pumpkin?!"

While Sally and Linus scanned the dark, pumpkin-filled horizon . . .

. . . the rest of the gang enjoyed a great Halloween party. They bobbed for apples and played games for prizes.

There were caramel apples, popcorn balls, jazzy music, and spooky decorations. Everyone had a fantastic time!

Meanwhile, in the pumpkin patch, Sally sighed. "If anyone had told me I'd be waiting in a pumpkin patch on Halloween night, I'd have said they were crazy."

"Just think, Sally, when the Great Pumpkin rises out of the pumpkin patch, we'll be here to see him," Linus replied.

And just then there was a rustling in the nearby pumpkin vines! Could it be? Was the Great Pumpkin finally going to appear?

Linus saw a dark shape rise. His heart pounded. . . .

And then Linus fainted!

Sally took a closer look at the dark figure. It wasn't the Great Pumpkin. It was Snoopy! The World War I Flying Ace had found shelter in an enemy pumpkin patch.

When Linus finally opened his eyes, he asked, "What happened? Did I see him? Did the Great Pumpkin leave us toys?"

But there were no toys. There had been no Great Pumpkin—just Charlie Brown's dog, Snoopy.

Sally wailed, "I was robbed! Halloween is over and I missed it. You kept me waiting all night and all that came was a beagle! I'll sue!"

After the party the trick-or-treaters stopped by the
pumpkin patch to check on Sally and Linus.
Sally was furious. But Linus still wasn't ready to give up.

"Hey, aren't you going to wait and greet the Great Pumpkin? It won't be long now!" Linus shouted.

The children just walked away. Sally left too.

"If the Great Pumpkin comes, I'll still put in a good word for you!" Linus called after them.

"Good grief, I said *if*, not *when!*" Linus cried.

"One little slip like that can cause the Great Pumpkin to pass you by," he said, fretting. "Oh, Great Pumpkin, where are you? . . ."

Ding-ding! Ding-ding! At four in the morning, Lucy's alarm clock chimed.

She got out of bed and went to Linus's room. As she expected, his bed was empty.

Lucy put on her coat and went to the
pumpkin patch. She found her little brother
shivering and alone. Once again, Linus had
missed Halloween.

36

Lucy brought her brother home, took off his muddy shoes, and tucked him in bed.
Another Halloween had come and gone—and the Great Pumpkin hadn't appeared.

The next day Charlie Brown tried to make Linus feel better. "Don't take it too hard. I've done a lot of stupid things in my life too."

"Waiting for the Great Pumpkin isn't stupid!" Linus replied. "Just wait until next year, Charlie Brown. You'll see. I'll find a pumpkin patch that's real sincere and I'll wait until the Great Pumpkin rises up . . ."

And who knows? Maybe next year . . .

A Charlie Brown
Thanksgiving

By Charles M. Schulz
Adapted by Justine and Ron Fontes
Art adapted by Tom Brannon
Based on the television special produced by Lee Mendelson and Bill Melendez

On Thanksgiving Day, Charlie Brown stood sadly at his mailbox
watching Snoopy walk off with a stack of mail—all for him!
Sally came up and asked, "What's the matter, big brother?"
"Nothing," Charlie Brown replied. "I was just checking the mailbox."
"What did you expect," Sally asked, "a turkey card?"

40

Charlie Brown sighed. "Holidays always depress me."

"I know what you mean," Sally said. "Why should I give thanks on Thanksgiving? What do I have to be thankful for?"

Linus walked up and asked, "What's all the commotion?"

"We've got another holiday to worry about," Charlie Brown grumbled. "Thanksgiving is here."

"I haven't even finished my Halloween candy," Sally wailed.

"Thanksgiving is important," Linus explained. "Our country was the first to make a national holiday to give thanks."

Sally looked at Linus and sighed and said, "Isn't he the cutest thing?"

When Charlie Brown and Sally went inside, the phone rang. It was Peppermint Patty.

"Listen, Chuck, I have a treat for you," she said. "My dad's been called out of town. He said I can join you for Thanksgiving."

Charlie Brown didn't know what to say. "Well . . . I . . ."

"I don't mind inviting myself because I know you kind of like me, Chuck," Peppermint Patty continued.

"Well . . . I . . ."

"Okay, it's a date," Peppermint Patty said. "See you soon, you sly devil."

43

"Oh, brother," Charlie Brown said. "Peppermint Patty's coming to Thanksgiving dinner."

"We won't even be home," Sally pointed out. "We'll be at Grandma's."

The phone rang. It was Peppermint Patty again.

"Hi, Chuck," she said. "Listen, I have even greater news. Remember that kid Marcie? Her folks said it would be okay if she joined us. So you can count on two for dinner, Chuck."

Charlie Brown said, "Well, the problem is . . ."

But Peppermint Patty talked right over him. "Don't worry, Chuck. We won't make problems. We'll help clean up dishes and everything. Just save me a drumstick and the neck. See you, Chuck."

Charlie Brown hung up the phone. "How do I get myself into these things?" he wailed. "Now she's bringing Marcie, too!"

"It's your own fault for being so wishy-washy," Sally said.

And before Charlie Brown could argue, Peppermint Patty called back yet again. This time she had invited Franklin to dinner too!

"I'm doomed!" Charlie Brown exclaimed. "Three guests for Thanksgiving, and I'm not even going to be home! Peppermint Patty will hate me for the rest of my life."

But Linus had a solution. "Why not have two dinners? You cook the first one for your friends, then go to your grandmother's for the second one."

"But I can't cook," Charlie Brown said. "All I can make is cold cereal and toast."

Linus was sure they could do it with a little help. He told Snoopy, "Go to the garage and get a table for the backyard."

Snoopy saluted, sharp as a soldier. The world's most brilliant beagle was on the case!

As Woodstock fluttered above him Snoopy dragged a Ping-Pong table out of the overflowing garage. As soon as Snoopy opened the table, it snapped shut! He was trapped inside!

SNAP!

When the beagle broke free, so did a Ping-Pong paddle and ball. Snoopy hit the ball, then bounced over the net so fast that he returned his own serve. Snoopy played against himself until he accidentally knocked Woodstock out.

Linus walked up just in time to see the end of Snoopy's game. "We don't have time to play," Linus scolded.

Snoopy blushed. Woodstock was awake again, but seeing stars.

"We still need some chairs around the table," Linus said, directing.

Once again, Snoopy bravely battled his way through the stuffed garage.
A lawn chair proved even tougher to unfold than the Ping-Pong table!
Finally Snoopy got everything under control. He even put a tablecloth
on the Ping-Pong table.

Then it was time to start cooking. With the precision of an army, Charlie Brown, Linus, Snoopy, and Woodstock used every toaster they could to make a big stack of buttered toast. The friends popped corn and opened bags of chips, pretzels, and jelly beans.

52

Next Snoopy set the table. He dealt the plates like a deck of cards and expertly folded the napkins into cute little tepees.

Yikes! One of the tepees moved. Snoopy carefully lifted the napkin and found . . . Woodstock!

Ding-dong!
The doorbell rang. Peppermint Patty, Marcie, and Franklin arrived. They followed Charlie Brown to the table in the backyard.

"Say, Chuck, this looks like quite a spread," said Peppermint Patty. "I bet this is one Thanksgiving dinner we'll *never* forget!"

Snoopy carried out a big domed platter.
"Aren't we going to say grace before we're served, Chuck?" Peppermint Patty asked. "It's Thanksgiving," she pointed out.

Charlie Brown wasn't sure what to do.

Linus came to the rescue. He stood up and gave a speech:

"In the year 1621, the Pilgrims had their first Thanksgiving feast. They invited the great Indian Chief Massasoit, who brought ninety of his brave Indians and a great abundance of food. Governor William Bradford and Captain Miles Standish were honored guests. Elder William Brewster, who was a minister, said a prayer that went something like this: We thank God for our homes and our food and our safety in a new land. We thank God for the opportunity to create a new world for freedom and justice!"

Peppermint Patty added, "Amen."

And with that, Snoopy lifted the lid to reveal their "feast."
He shuffled the toast like cards, then plunked a piece onto a
paper plate. He added a pawful of popcorn, pretzel sticks, and
jelly beans. Then he threw the plate like a Frisbee across the table.
Zoom, zoom, zoom! Plates flew to each guest.

Peppermint Patty stared in amazed disappointment. "What kind of Thanksgiving is this?!" she asked. "Don't you know anything about cooking a real Thanksgiving dinner, Chuck? Where's the turkey? Where are the mashed potatoes, cranberry sauce, and pumpkin pie? What blockhead made all this?"

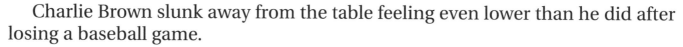

Charlie Brown slunk away from the table feeling even lower than he did after losing a baseball game.

Marcie turned to Peppermint Patty. "You were kinda rough on Charles, weren't you, sir? Did he invite you to dinner, or did you invite yourself?"

"I never thought of it like that," Peppermint Patty admitted. "Do you think I hurt ol' Chuck's feelings? Golly, why can't I act right outside of a baseball game?"

Peppermint Patty convinced Marcie to apologize for her. When Marcie found Charlie Brown inside the house she said, "Don't feel bad, Charles. Peppermint Patty didn't mean all those things she said. Actually, she really likes you."

"I don't feel bad for myself," Charlie Brown explained. "I'm just sorry I ruined everyone's Thanksgiving."

"But Thanksgiving is more than eating, Charles. You heard what Linus said. The Pilgrims were thankful, and we should be thankful for just being together," Marcie said.

Peppermint Patty had been listening from the doorway. She came in and offered Charlie Brown her hand. "Apologies accepted, Chuck?" They shook hands.

Peppermint Patty continued, "There are enough problems in the world already without these silly misunderstandings." Suddenly she grinned. "Why, you're holding my hand, you sly dog."

BONG! BONG! BONG! BONG! The clock chimed. Good grief! Four o'clock already!

"We're supposed to be at Grandmother's house at four thirty," Charlie Brown said, fretting.

"I better call her and explain my dilemma." Charlie Brown picked up the phone. "Hello? Gran'ma? This is Chuck, I mean, Charlie Brown. We're going to be a little late." Then he explained about his friends still being there. "No, ma'am, they haven't eaten. As a matter of fact, they've let me know that in no uncertain terms!" Then Charlie Brown heard some wonderful news.

Marcie announced it to the rest of the gang. "We're all invited to Charlie Brown's grandmother's for Thanksgiving dinner!"

The kids all cheered!

Soon the whole gang, except for Snoopy and Woodstock, piled into the back of the station wagon.

In the car, the kids sang, "*Over the river and through the woods, to grandmother's house we go! The horse knows the way to carry the sleigh through the white and drifting snow . . . oh—*"

Charlie Brown interrupted the happy tune. "There's only one thing wrong with that."
Linus asked, "What's that, Charlie Brown?"
"My grandmother lives in a condominium."
But then he realized that it doesn't matter *where* you eat Thanksgiving dinner.
Whether it's at a condo . . .

. . . or at a doghouse, it will always be special when you share the feast with friends.

A Charlie Brown Christmas

By Charles M. Schulz
Adapted by Justine and Ron Fontes
Art adapted by Paige Braddock
Based on the television special produced by Lee Mendelson and Bill Melendez

Snowflakes floated in the crisp, pine-scented air. The wind carried the joyful sounds of jingling bells, Christmas carols, and people wishing one another happy holidays.

The greatest time of the year was finally here! Whipping across a frozen pond, the Peanuts gang was as happy as, well, children at Christmastime—all except good ol' Charlie Brown.

"I think there's something wrong with me," Charlie Brown told Linus. "I just don't understand Christmas. I like getting presents, sending cards, decorating trees, and all that. But I always end up feeling sad."

Linus sighed. "You're the only person I know who could turn a wonderful season like Christmas into a problem. Maybe Lucy's right. Of all the Charlie Browns in the world, you are the Charlie Browniest."

Charlie Brown felt even sadder when he opened his empty mailbox. "Rats! Nobody sent me a Christmas card today. I know nobody likes me. But why does the holiday season have to rub it in?"

Charlie Brown felt so depressed, he decided to see his psychiatrist, Lucy. He dropped a nickel in her can and sighed. "I just don't understand Christmas. Instead of feeling happy, I feel sort of let down."

"You need to get involved!" Lucy exclaimed. She knew just how to get her patient into the Christmas spirit. "How would you like to direct our Christmas play? I'll meet you at the theater."

Charlie Brown decided to give it a try. After all, things couldn't get much worse.

PSYCHIATRIC
HELP 5¢

THE DOCTOR
IS REAL IN

On his way to the theater, Charlie Brown passed his dog. Snoopy was decorating his doghouse with heaps of shiny ornaments.

"What's going on here?" Charlie Brown asked.

Snoopy showed him a flyer.

Find the true meaning of Christmas. Win MONEY, MONEY, MONEY.
Enter the Christmas lights and display contest!

"My own dog has gone commercial," Charlie Brown wailed. "I can't stand it!" He was sick of all the greedy buying and selling that had become Christmas.

Helping his little sister, Sally, write a letter to Santa only made Charlie Brown feel worse.

"I have been extra good this year, so enclosed is an extra-long list of things I want," Sally began.

"Good grief!" Charlie Brown's stomach hurt. What had happened to giving and sharing?

"Or perhaps you should just send money," Sally concluded. "I would prefer tens and twenties."

But Charlie Brown did not have time to lecture Sally about the meaning of Christmas. He had a show to direct! He hurried to the theater.

"Let's get down to work," Charlie Brown told the cast. "It's the spirit of the actors that counts, the interest they show in their director. Am I right? I said, 'Am I right?'"

But nobody was listening. They were all dancing to Schroeder's bouncy piano music.

Ba-ba-da-ba ba-da-ba-bum-daaa-dum.

"Stop the music!" Charlie Brown shouted. Then he told Lucy to hand out the scripts and costumes.

"Do innkeepers' wives have naturally curly hair?" Frieda wondered.

Pigpen promised to keep a clean inn.

Sherman complained, "Every year I play a shepherd."

Snoopy agreed to be all the animals—even some that weren't in the play!

Lucy came up with five good reasons for Linus to learn his lines and "get rid of that stupid blanket!" But Linus found a way to keep his blanket in the show.

The rehearsal went about as well as one of Charlie Brown's baseball games.
Frieda worried that Pigpen's dust was ruining her curls. Lucy called for a
lunch break. Linus hid under his blanket.
And instead of listening to their director, everyone danced to Schroeder's jazz.
Ba-ba-da-ba ba-da-ba-bum-daaa-dum.

Frustrated, Charlie Brown finally cried out, "That does it!"

Lucy stopped snapping her fingers and asked, "What's the matter, Charlie Brown?"

"This Christmas play is all wrong!" he wailed.

Lucy tried to calm him. "Let's face it. We all know Christmas is just a racket set up to make people buy lots of stuff they don't need."

Charlie Brown shook his head. "This is one play that won't be like that. We need the proper mood. What we need is . . . a Christmas tree!"

"That's it, Charlie Brown! We need a great, big, shiny aluminum tree!" Lucy exclaimed. "You get the tree. I'll handle this crowd," she said, taking charge of bossing everyone around.

"I'll take Linus with me," Charlie Brown said. "The rest of you can practice your lines."

"Get the biggest aluminum tree you can find, maybe painted pink!" Lucy added.

Charlie Brown felt a familiar knot in his stomach. "I don't know, Linus. I just don't know," he said, sighing as the two boys walked to the Christmas tree lot.

Soon they were surrounded by a fantastic forest of fake trees. Some were plastic or pink or even polka-dotted!

84

"Gee, do they still make wooden Christmas trees?" Linus wondered aloud.

Then Charlie Brown pointed to a tiny tree barely strong enough to hold on to its needles. He said, "This little one seems to need a home."

Linus worried about what Lucy would think. But Charlie Brown bought the tiny tree anyway.

"What kind of tree is that?" they shrieked when the boys got back to the theater with the scrawny tree. "You were supposed to get a good tree!"

"You're hopeless, Charlie Brown, completely hopeless," Violet scolded.

Everyone laughed at the skinny tree—even Snoopy!
Charlie Brown's heart sank. "I guess you were right, Linus. I shouldn't have picked this little tree. I guess I really don't know what Christmas is about," he wailed. "Isn't there anyone who knows what Christmas is all about?"

"Sure, Charlie Brown. I can tell you what Christmas is about."

Linus stepped into the spotlight and said: "And there were shepherds, abiding in the field keeping watch over their flock by night. And the Angel of the Lord came upon them and said, 'Fear not: for behold, I bring you tidings of great joy. For unto you is born this day a Savior, which is Christ the Lord.' And there was with the angel a multitude of heavenly hosts praising God and saying, 'Glory to God; peace on Earth, good will to men.'

"That is what Christmas is all about, Charlie Brown."

Suddenly, Charlie Brown
didn't care what anyone
thought of him or his tree.
He finally felt happy, the
way he was supposed to
feel at Christmas!

Charlie Brown stepped out into the cold, silent night and looked up at the twinkling stars.

"Linus is right. I won't let all this greed spoil my Christmas. I'll decorate this little tree and show everyone it really will work in our play."

Charlie Brown took a bright, red ball off Snoopy's prize-winning doghouse. He hung the ball on the tiny tree. The tree slowly bent over until its top touched the ground.

That was all it took to spoil Charlie Brown's mood.
"Argh! I've killed it! Everything I touch gets ruined!"
Charlie Brown walked away with his shoulders as
bent as the little tree's trunk.

After Charlie Brown had left, the others found the tree.

"It's not a bad little tree, really," Linus said. He wrapped his blanket around its base. "It just needs a little love."

The rest of the gang helped. In a flash Snoopy's doghouse decorations had transformed the tree.

The children gathered around the pretty little tree and hummed "O Little Town of Bethlehem."

They could almost see the shepherds guarding their flocks by night.

When Charlie Brown returned to the group, he could hardly believe his eyes.

"What's going on here?" he shouted.
How had the tree become so beautiful? Charlie
Brown's heart filled with joy when he realized
what everyone had done for his tree. It was a
Christmas miracle.

Linus, Lucy, and the rest of the gang smiled and shouted, "Merry Christmas, Charlie Brown!"

And for Charlie Brown, it truly was the merriest Christmas ever.

Be My Valentine, Charlie Brown

By Charles M. Schulz
Adapted by Justine and Ron Fontes
Art adapted by Vincent Martone
Based on the television special produced by Lee Mendelson and Bill Melendez

Valentine's Day was almost here, and Charlie Brown still hadn't received a single card! Nobody ever sent him a valentine, but that didn't stop Charlie Brown from hoping his luck would change.

"What are you doing, Charlie Brown?" Lucy asked.

"I'm waiting for valentines," he explained.

"Oh . . . well, good luck," Lucy replied. "You'll need it."

Every year was the same. When the gang went trick-or-treating for Halloween, Charlie Brown always got a rock. And on Valentine's Day he got nothing! But maybe this year would be different. Charlie Brown reached deep into the mailbox and found . . . nothing! There wasn't even junk mail.

Charlie Brown wasn't the only one with romance on his mind. Linus pined for his pretty teacher, Miss Othmar.

"Did you hear? She said my name! I think Miss Othmar really likes me," Linus said, gushing.

"Don't be ridiculous, Linus," Sally said. "Miss Othmar was calling the roll. To her, you're just another student." Sally was jealous. Her sweet baboo wasn't supposed to have a crush on someone else.

But Linus was sure Miss Othmar liked him—especially when she asked him to clean the erasers.

"It's an honor to pound erasers," he told Sally.

Linus pounded with all his might. The chalk dust flew off in great white clouds that made him gag.

"I could choke from all this honor."

After school Charlie Brown reached into his empty mailbox again. "I could spend my whole life here and never get a valentine," he complained.

"That's it!" Linus exclaimed. "I'll get Miss Othmar the best valentine ever. That'll show her how I feel about her."

Linus hurried to the store and bought the biggest box of candy he could afford.

When Violet saw the huge box she cried, "Wow! A heart-shaped box of candy!"

Linus explained, "This is my valentine for Miss Othmar."

"It's kind of expensive, isn't it?" Violet asked.

"The amount of money you spend on a present should equal the affection you have for that person," Linus declared.

"It's not a good idea to fall in love with your teacher," Violet cautioned.

"I didn't say I was in love," Linus pointed out. "I'm merely very fond of the ground on which she walks."

Linus left the store with a big smile on his face. He didn't even notice Sally, but Sally saw him!

"Did you see that big box of candy Linus bought for me?" Sally asked Violet. "It's fantastic! I'll have to get a good present for him, too!"

Sally was busy thinking about what to buy her sweet baboo, and she hurried off before Violet had a chance to explain that the candy wasn't for her.

All the students were looking forward to the school Valentine's Day party. Schroeder was in charge, and he explained how the card box worked.

"Each pupil will drop their valentines into the box. Then I'll give them out at the party," Schroeder said.

Sally raised her hand. "Can the valentines be homemade?"

Schroeder and Miss Othmar agreed that homemade valentines could be very special.

Charlie Brown was excited. "Boy, here's my chance!" he said to himself. "In this big class someone is sure to give me a valentine!"

Sally couldn't wait to make a special valentine for Linus. But she soon wailed, "I can't fold! I can't cut! I can't paste!"

Charlie Brown showed Sally how to cut out a paper heart. But when she tried, Sally wound up with a clover, and then a diamond!

Snoopy folded a piece of paper over and over, made a few crisp snips with the scissors, and unfolded the paper. Snoopy's valentine was amazing. It even played music!

"You can do that too," Charlie Brown told Sally. He folded a piece of paper over and over. "Just cut out some diamonds, hearts, and moons." He unfolded the paper—and it crumbled into a heap of scraps.

Charlie Brown made valentines all night!
The next day, he walked into school with his
hands full of valentines and his heart full of hope.
Charlie Brown also carried an empty briefcase, so the
valentines he received wouldn't get wrinkled on the
way home.

112

In the classroom, Schroeder announced, "Okay, everybody! It's time to put your valentines in the box. Then we'll have our party and refreshments." All the kids hurried to put their valentines in the box.

"Did you see my name on any?" Charlie Brown asked.

"I haven't been paying attention," Schroeder said. "What's the briefcase for?"

"If I get lots of valentines, I'll need something to carry them in," Charlie Brown explained. Now he wondered if his briefcase would be big enough. He liked to be prepared.

Linus couldn't fit the big heart full of chocolates into the card box. "Is it all right if I deliver my valentine personally?" he asked.

Miss Othmar said it would be delightful.

Linus floated back to his seat. "She said it would be delightful! This is going to be better than I expected."

Sally was excited too. She gave Linus her homemade valentine. "Thanks," Linus said as he tossed it on his desk without a second glance. Sally waited, but Linus didn't give her the big box of candy.

What happened? she wondered. *He forgot to give me my box of candy. Maybe he's bashful,* Sally reasoned. *He'll give it to me later, and I'll give him a big smooch.*

Soon Schroeder announced it was time to start passing out the valentines. Charlie Brown wondered if he should have brought two briefcases, just to be sure.

Schroeder called out lots of names—but not Charlie Brown's! Charlie Brown kept waiting . . . and waiting!

VvWwXxYyZz

"Has there been a mistake?" Charlie Brown asked. "Is there one for me?"

"No, Charlie Brown. When I get one with your name, I'll let you know," Schroeder assured him.

Charlie Brown sighed.

Violet said, "Look at that! Charlie Brown still hasn't received a valentine. Did anyone send him a valentine?"

"Who would waste a valentine on him?" Lucy replied.

Charlie Brown took a candy heart from the bowl. Instead of SWEET BABY or BE MINE, his candy said FORGET IT, KID.

When all the valentines had been passed out, Charlie Brown checked the empty box. He turned it upside down. But there were still no valentines for him.

120

Linus decided it was time to give Miss Othmar her valentine. But the teacher wasn't at her desk.

"She left for the parking lot a minute ago," Schroeder said.

Linus rushed to the door.

Sally saw Linus coming and cried, "This is the big moment! My lover boy approaches with my valentine!" She closed her eyes and puckered up for a kiss. But when she opened her eyes, Linus was gone! "Where did he go with my box of candy?" she asked.

"Linus went after Miss Othmar," Violet said.
"I just saw Miss Othmar with her boyfriend," Charlie Brown added.
"He's running to Miss Othmar's car with my box of candy!" Sally wailed.

The car pulled away just as Linus ran up. He hid his tears behind the big red box. Miss Othmar had her own Valentine's Day plans—with someone else!

His heart broken, Linus walked to a stone bridge. He pulled the wrapper off the box and cried, "I spent all of my money on this valentine. I made a fool of myself!"

Then he threw the chocolates one by one over the bridge. "This is for love. This is for valentines. This is for romance. . . ."

Below the bridge, Snoopy and Woodstock caught the delicious candies in their mouths.

Charlie Brown felt just as bad as Linus on Valentine's Day.
But the next morning, he got his hopes up all over again. "Maybe
I did get a valentine. Maybe it just didn't get here until today!
Maybe it's in the mailbox right now!"

Charlie Brown ran to open his mailbox—and Snoopy
popped out and kissed him on the nose! Charlie Brown slammed
the mailbox shut and shouted, "I hate Valentine's Day!"

Just then the whole gang showed up.

"We've been feeling awfully guilty about not giving you a valentine, Charlie Brown," Violet explained. "I've erased my name from this one, and I'd like you to have it."

Schroeder shrieked, "Where were you yesterday?! Don't you think he has any feelings? You don't really care about Charlie Brown. You just hate feeling guilty. You have the nerve to offer him a used valentine? Well, let me tell you something. Charlie Brown doesn't need your—"

"Don't listen to him!" Charlie Brown shouted, snatching the card gratefully. Deep down, his friends did care. Even a used valentine was better than none at all!

127

The big day was over, but at least Charlie Brown and Linus had each other.

"I guess I let Schroeder down by accepting Violet's used card. But it was my first valentine. And at least they showed a little thought for me. Maybe this is the start of a trend." His voice soared with hope. "Maybe next year I'll get a whole bunch of valentines! Maybe I'll need three briefcases!"

Linus looked at his cheerful friend and sighed. Charlie Brown would never change. "Happy Valentine's Day, Charlie Brown!"

It's the Easter Beagle, Charlie Brown!

By Charles M. Schulz
Adapted by Justine and Ron Fontes
Art adapted by Paige Braddock
Based on the television special produced by Lee Mendelson and Bill Melendez

The winter snow had melted. Flowers were in bloom. The entire Peanuts gang was getting ready for Easter!

Peppermint Patty was teaching her friend Marcie how to decorate Easter eggs.

"I got the eggs, sir, just like you asked," Marcie said.

"You get the eggs ready, and I'll mix up all the colors," Peppermint Patty said. "And please stop calling me sir!"

While Peppermint Patty was busy with the dyes, Marcie cooked the eggs. "All the eggs are fried, sir. Now, how do we color them?" she asked.

Peppermint Patty and Marcie weren't the only ones with Easter problems. Sally didn't see how she could celebrate without new shoes.

Linus and Lucy needed eggs, baskets, and candy. "Want to go to the store with us, Sally?" Lucy asked.

"I told you, it's a waste of time," Linus said. "The Easter Beagle takes care of all that."

"Linus, you drive me crazy!" Lucy cried.

132

But Sally was curious. "Who's the Easter Beagle?" she asked. "Sally," Linus explained, "we don't need to go to all this trouble. On Easter Sunday the Easter Beagle comes dancing along, passing out colored eggs to all the good little kids."

Charlie Brown sighed. His sister had been fooled before by Linus's holiday heroes. "Come on, Sally, I thought you wanted to get some new shoes."

At the store Charlie Brown, Sally, Linus, Lucy, and Snoopy met Peppermint Patty and Marcie.

"Hi, Chuck! What are you up to? We're here to get some eggs to color for Easter," Peppermint Patty said. "Marcie here fried the last batch." Then she whispered, "This kid doesn't quite get it, Chuck."

"It's a waste of time to buy and color eggs," Linus said, "because the Easter Beagle will do all that."

Peppermint Patty rolled her eyes. "Boy, Chuck, you sure have some strange friends. But c'mon, let's go buy some eggs. Easter Beagle, indeed!"

Sally found a pair of blue, high-heeled shoes. She couldn't walk in them, but they sure were different!

Snoopy found a hollow Easter egg. He looked inside and saw bunnies dancing.

Snoopy imagined dancing with the bunnies. His feet felt as light as flower petals, and his heart was full of Easter joy! The bunnies applauded his happy dance.

Linus kept trying to convince his friends to believe in the Easter Beagle.

Lucy lost her patience. "Good grief! There's no Easter Beagle!" she declared.

Sally wanted to believe Linus, but she had been disappointed before. "This sounds faintly familiar. I remember sitting in a stupid pumpkin patch all night waiting for the Great Pumpkin."

"This is different," Linus explained. "That was Halloween. This is Easter. The Easter Beagle will *never* let you down," he insisted.

"Well," said Sally slowly, "I really want to believe you, because I like you. But I just don't know."

Marcie and Peppermint Patty brought their freshly bought eggs back to Peppermint Patty's kitchen. This time Marcie was sure she was cooking the eggs right. She put some in the waffle iron! Then she tried to put one in the toaster! When that didn't work, Marcie used the oven.

AARGH!

Once again Marcie had ruined all the eggs! Peppermint Patty's sandals slapped the sidewalk as she stomped back to the store. At this rate, they'd finish making Easter eggs in July!

On the way they met Linus.

"Hi! Where are you going in such a hurry?" Linus asked.

"We keep running out of eggs," Peppermint Patty complained. "I'm still trying to show Marcie how to color eggs for Easter Sunday."

"You're making a mistake," Linus reminded them. "On Easter Sunday the Easter Beagle brings eggs to all the good little children."

"Sir, is this right?" Marcie asked. "Perhaps we don't have to go to all this trouble. If this Easter Beagle—"

Peppermint Patty sighed. "Kid, I'm having enough problems without your crazy stories. C'mon, Marcie, let's get another dozen."

"It's a waste of time!" Linus called after them.

When they got back to the kitchen Peppermint Patty told Marcie exactly how to cook the eggs. "These eggs are not to be fried, roasted, toasted, or waffled. These eggs must be boiled."
Marcie filled a pot with water and turned on the flame.
"Put the eggs in now. When the water comes to a boil let me know," Peppermint Patty said.

142

Marcie cracked the eggs into the pot one by one. "Okay, sir, all the eggs are in."

"Good, Marcie. Let them boil a long time. Then I'll show you how to paint them," Peppermint Patty told her.

After awhile Marcie said, "The eggs look done, sir."

On the way to the stove Peppermint Patty sniffed the air. "That's funny. It smells like soup," she said.

Peppermint Patty looked into the pot and cried, "You made egg soup! Arrrgh!"

Peppermint Patty didn't know what to do, so she complained to her friends. "We don't have enough money for more eggs. How can I teach Marcie about Easter?"

Once again Linus reminded the gang: "Don't worry. The Easter Beagle will bring eggs to all the good little kids, and everyone will be filled with great joy."

Peppermint Patty sighed. "Kid, I hope you're right." Her egg-dyeing days were over!

No matter what Linus said, Lucy wasn't counting on the Easter Beagle. She made her very own Easter eggs for her own Easter egg hunt.

"You're wasting your time," Linus cried.

"Leave me alone!" Lucy said. "Don't bother me with your stupid ideas." She had a practical Easter plan that was guaranteed to work. "Easter is very simple," she explained. "You paint the eggs. You hide the eggs. You find the eggs. And you know who's going to find them? Me! Because I'm the one who's going to *hide* them."

When all her eggs were colored, Lucy put them in a big basket and took them to the field where the Easter celebration would take place. Each time she hid an egg, she wrote down where she put it.

Lucy couldn't wait for Easter Sunday. She was going to have the greatest Easter egg hunt ever!

On Easter morning Peppermint Patty and Marcie went to the field for their big party. Peppermint Patty apologized to her friend. "I'm sorry we don't have any Easter eggs, Marcie."

"I'm the one who's sorry, sir," Marcie replied. "I guess I'm not much of a cook."

Peppermint Patty sighed. "I've seen this happen on holidays before. You look forward to being really happy. Then something happens that spoils it all."

Charlie Brown knew just what Peppermint Patty meant. To him, every holiday was just another day to be disappointed. "I know why they have holidays: so people can get together and have fun," Charlie Brown sighed. "So why am I alone?"

150

Sally was also unhappy. She scolded Linus. "I've been waiting for the Easter Beagle since dawn. Where is he?!" She had that pumpkin-patch feeling all over again.

"Why do I listen to you? 'Trust me,' you said. Now I've been burned again. Never trust a man with a blanket," she fumed. "Get me my lawyer!"

151

Suddenly the Easter Beagle danced into view in the field behind Linus and Lucy's house! Over his arm he carried a bright basket brimming with colorful eggs. His feet were as light as flower petals. His smile was pure joy!

"The Easter Beagle is coming!" Linus cried with delight.
All the children stared in amazement at this wonderful vision of spring!

The Easter Beagle tossed eggs to Peppermint Patty, Marcie, Linus, and Sally. "Thank you, Easter Beagle!" Linus cried.

The Easter Beagle gave eggs to Schroeder and Lucy. He even tossed an egg into Woodstock's birdhouse. And wherever his dancing feet touched the ground, joy sprang up like daffodils on the first day of spring.

But by the time he reached Charlie Brown the Easter Beagle's basket was empty.

Charlie Brown sighed. Of course he wouldn't get anything. He never did. Nothing but rocks on Halloween, no cards on Valentine's Day, and now no eggs on Easter. No matter what day it was, he was still Charlie Brown.

"What do we do with our Easter eggs now that we have them, sir?" Marcie wondered.

"Put a little salt on them and eat them," Peppermint Patty replied.

Marcie salted her egg then bit into it, shell and all. *CRUNCH!* "Tastes terrible, sir."

Peppermint Patty could not believe her sweet, clueless friend. Marcie was lovable, but she just didn't get it!

"See, Linus was right. There *is* an Easter Beagle," Sally said.

Lucy looked at the striped egg that Snoopy had given her. It looked very familiar. "Some Easter Beagle," she scoffed. "He gave me my own egg!"

Lucy was furious! She had painted and hidden those eggs, and *she* was supposed to find them all!

"Why don't you go talk to the Easter Beagle?" Linus suggested.

Lucy decided to confront Snoopy at his doghouse. "Put up your dukes!" she cried.
Lucy was ready for a fight. Instead, Snoopy popped out of his doghouse and kissed her!
Suddenly Lucy felt all the giddy joy of spring. For once Linus was right about something. Easter meant flowers, fun, and most of all . . . the Easter Beagle!